For Luke Sorby, Kerry
and Paul's own miracle
– M.H.

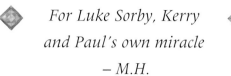 *For Catherine and Sam,*
with much love
– J.M.

First published in the United States
by Phyllis Fogelman Books
An imprint of Penguin Putnam Books for Young Readers
345 Hudson Street
New York, New York 10014

Published in the United Kingdom
by Frances Lincoln Limited, 4 Torriano Mews
Torriano Avenue, London NW5 2RZ
Text copyright © 2001 by Mary Hoffman
Pictures copyright © 2001 by Jackie Morris
All rights reserved
Printed in Singapore

1 3 5 7 9 10 8 6 4 2

Library of Congress Cataloging-in-Publication Data
available upon request

Mary Hoffman ◆ Jackie Morris

Miracles

◆ WONDERS JESUS WORKED ◆

PHYLLIS FOGELMAN BOOKS

NEW PJF YORK

CONTENTS

INTRODUCTION

What is a miracle? It looks a lot like magic. For a miracle to happen, at least one of the laws of nature has to be overturned. Jesus could walk on water, cure people without even meeting them, feed thousands with a few odds and ends, and control the weather. And in the greatest miracle of all, he brought someone who had died back to life.

Christians believe that Jesus was both human and God—so he could do anything. But he didn't do anything to save himself from his own cruel death. That is in some ways more marvelous than any miracle.

The stories of Jesus' miracles are some of the most famous in the Bible—the feeding of the five thousand, the bulging net of fishes, stilling the storm. I have chosen nine of them, ranging from what John tells us was Jesus' first miracle—turning water into wine—to the raising of his good friend Lazarus from the dead.

And it was the last miracle that sealed Jesus' fate. No one who was rumored to have such power over life and death could be allowed to live.

Mary M Hoffman

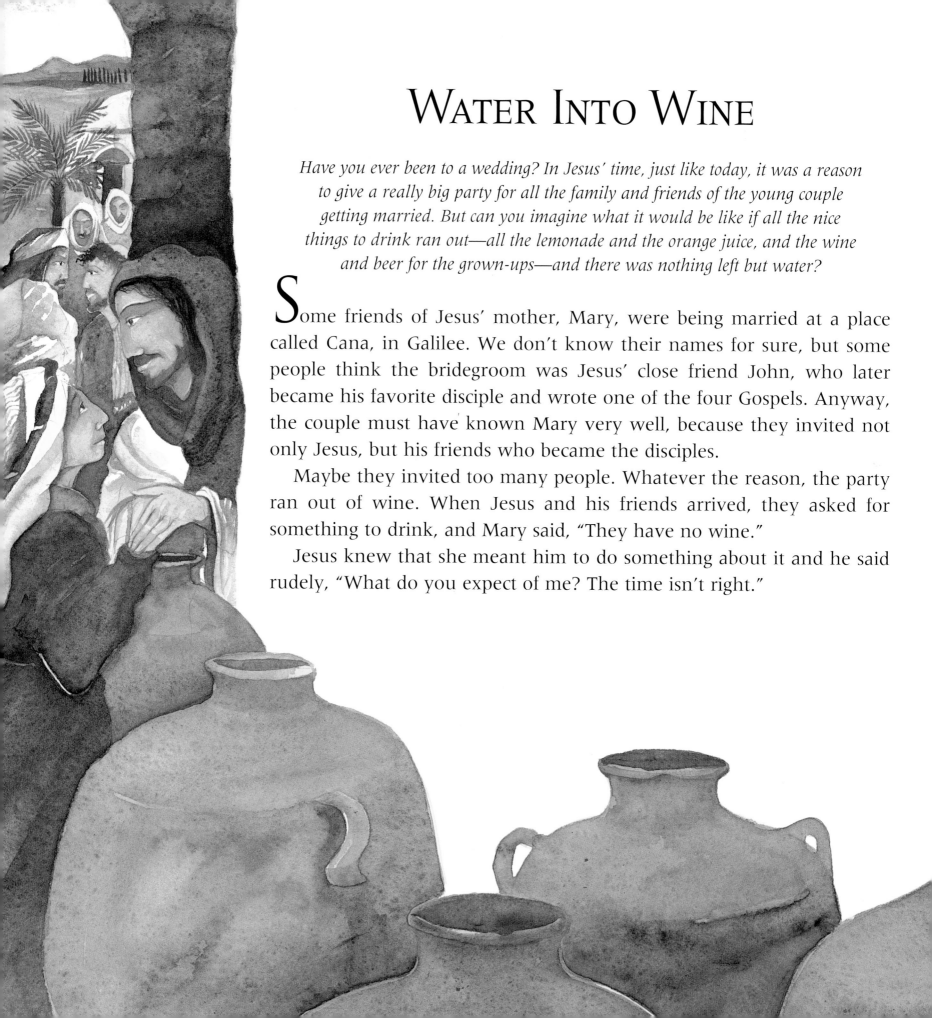

WATER INTO WINE

Have you ever been to a wedding? In Jesus' time, just like today, it was a reason to give a really big party for all the family and friends of the young couple getting married. But can you imagine what it would be like if all the nice things to drink ran out—all the lemonade and the orange juice, and the wine and beer for the grown-ups—and there was nothing left but water?

Some friends of Jesus' mother, Mary, were being married at a place called Cana, in Galilee. We don't know their names for sure, but some people think the bridegroom was Jesus' close friend John, who later became his favorite disciple and wrote one of the four Gospels. Anyway, the couple must have known Mary very well, because they invited not only Jesus, but his friends who became the disciples.

Maybe they invited too many people. Whatever the reason, the party ran out of wine. When Jesus and his friends arrived, they asked for something to drink, and Mary said, "They have no wine."

Jesus knew that she meant him to do something about it and he said rudely, "What do you expect of me? The time isn't right."

WEATHERMASTER

Have you ever been caught in a really bad thunderstorm? It can be terrifying. Lots of people are scared of thunder and lightning, even when they are grown up. But imagine how much worse it would be if you were in a little boat on the open sea.

Many of Jesus' friends were fishermen, and he often traveled in their fishing boats. One day, when he was tired after preaching to large crowds, he asked some friends to take him and his disciples in their ship to the other side of the lake known as the Sea of Galilee.

As soon as he came on board the ship, Jesus went into the stern, where he settled down on a pillow and fell deeply asleep.

But while Jesus slept, a storm blew up over the water. Big black clouds swept across the sky, and large, heavy drops of rain fell on the deck, but Jesus still slept. The wind whipped the water into huge waves, and the little boat was tossed up and down and from side to side. The waves smashed down over the sides of the ship so that it filled with water. But Jesus slept on.

The disciples were terrified. They had never known a storm like it. They frantically baled water out from the bottom of the ship. But it was no good: The boat was sinking.

"We're going to drown!" cried one. "Quick, wake up Jesus! He's the only one who can save us!"

Jesus woke, refreshed, and looked at his rain-soaked

A NETFUL of FISH

Have you ever tried to catch a fish? It's not that easy. Whether you use a rod or a net, fish are very quick and slippery. Jesus had many friends who caught fish for a living. When they caught a lot, they sold them for good money. But on some days they couldn't catch any.

When Jesus first began to tell people about God, crowds gathered to hear him. So Jesus asked his friend Simon Peter, who was a fisherman, if he could use his boat. He got into the boat and Simon Peter took it out a little way from the shore. Everyone settled down on the bank, while Jesus sat in the boat and told them the good news about God's love.

When he had finished, he said to Simon Peter, "Launch out further into the lake and let down your nets."

Simon said, "Master, we have been trying to catch fish all night. There are none to be had. But if you want, I shall let down the nets."

So he did—and he immediately felt the nets straining. He could scarcely haul them on board because they were filled to the brim with shoals of silvery fishes. There were so many that Simon Peter's nets couldn't hold them and they broke, spilling lots of fish back into the sea.

Simon Peter called out to his friends James and John, who were also out fishing on the lake. "Come and help! There are enough fish for all of us!"

That night they caught so many fish that both boats were full and in danger of sinking under the load.

When he saw the amazing quantities of fish, Simon Peter was ashamed that he had doubted Jesus' advice, and said, "I am not worthy to follow you."

Jesus just laughed, and said, "From now on, my friend, it will be people you catch, not fish."

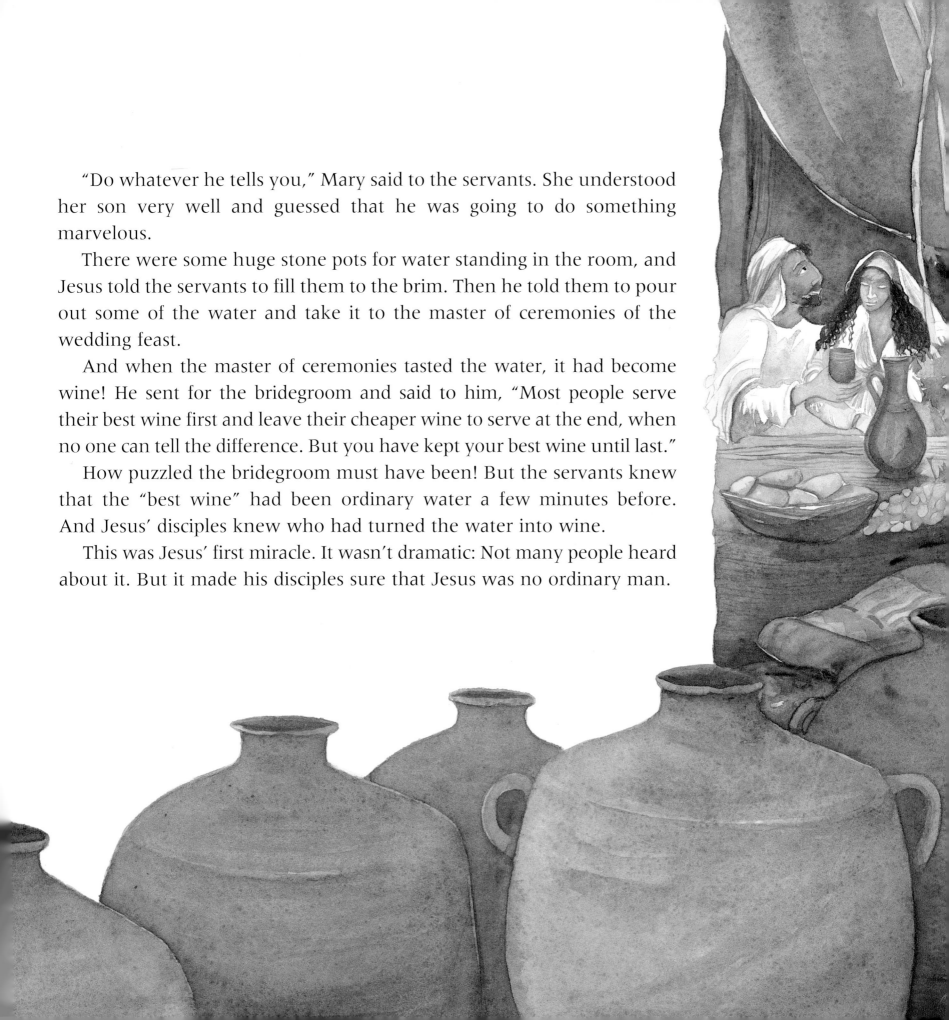

"Do whatever he tells you," Mary said to the servants. She understood her son very well and guessed that he was going to do something marvelous.

There were some huge stone pots for water standing in the room, and Jesus told the servants to fill them to the brim. Then he told them to pour out some of the water and take it to the master of ceremonies of the wedding feast.

And when the master of ceremonies tasted the water, it had become wine! He sent for the bridegroom and said to him, "Most people serve their best wine first and leave their cheaper wine to serve at the end, when no one can tell the difference. But you have kept your best wine until last."

How puzzled the bridegroom must have been! But the servants knew that the "best wine" had been ordinary water a few minutes before. And Jesus' disciples knew who had turned the water into wine.

This was Jesus' first miracle. It wasn't dramatic: Not many people heard about it. But it made his disciples sure that Jesus was no ordinary man.

and trembling friends. He shook his head. "How little faith you have!" he said.

Then he stood up in the boat and raised his arms. He spoke sternly to the storm, but the disciples couldn't hear his words for the howling of the wind and the driving rain. Immediately the wind dropped, the rain stopped, and the water became as calm as a pond.

The men on board the ship were even more frightened by the calm than by the storm.

"What kind of man is this," they asked, "if even the winds and waves obey him?"

THROUGH the ROOF

*Have you ever wished that you could make someone better?
If you have a friend or someone in your family who is very ill,
you want that person to be cured as soon as possible. When
the word got around that Jesus could perform miracles,
all the people who were ill came to look for him.*

Jesus was with his disciples in a house in Capernaum when word got around that he was there. First, one or two sick people came to ask him to make them better. Then more and more came to the house, and soon there were crowds clamoring to get in.

The sitting room was full to overflowing, and people spilled out onto the street. And still more sick people kept coming, in the hope that this miracle-worker could cure them. There were some teachers of law in the neighborhood who were watching what was going on.

Four men came along, carrying a friend of theirs on a makeshift bed. Now, this friend had been paralyzed for a long time and couldn't walk. He was full of hope that Jesus could make him better.

But when the four friends reached the house with their burden, they saw that there was no chance of getting in.

"What shall we do?" said one.

"We can't go back without seeing Jesus—we've come so far," said another.

"Let's try the roof!" said a third.

So the four friends climbed, with great difficulty, up onto the roof of the house where Jesus was, carrying the

bed and trying not to hurt their sick friend. When they got to the top, they made a hole in the roof. Then they lowered their friend very gently through the hole.

Imagine the surprise of Jesus and his disciples when they saw a bed descending from the ceiling, with a helpless man in it!

Jesus realized right away how great these people's faith in him was. He went to the paralyzed man and said, "Your sins are forgiven."

Everyone was shocked, especially the teachers of law, who were listening carefully. They had expected him to say something like "You are better now." Jesus knew this. He said to them, "Which do you think is easier to say: 'Your sins are forgiven,' or 'Take up your bed and walk'?"

No one answered. Jesus said, "The son of man can do both."

Then he turned to the sick man and said, "Get up, pick up your bed, and walk out of here on your own."

And the paralyzed man rose to his feet, picked up his bed, and walked steadily to the door. His friends peered down through the hole in the roof in amazement.

But the teachers of law muttered to one another, "Who does he think he is? Only God can forgive sins."

These were powerful men, and their disapproval meant danger for Jesus.

THE BIGGEST PICNIC in the WORLD

Have you ever been in a really big crowd of people? Today, whenever large numbers of people gather together in a theme park or at a pop festival, there are lots of vans and stalls and cafés selling fast food. But by the shores of Lake Galilee there was nothing but rocks and grass.

The more Jesus spoke to the people, the more people turned up to hear him. He spoke like no other preacher they had ever heard. He told them that God loved them and would forgive them their sins. And he healed people who had been blind or deaf or unable to walk since they were born.

Soon, wherever Jesus went, a huge crowd of people began to follow him. He was talking to such a crowd one hot and dusty day. When he finished speaking, one of his disciples came to him and said, "Lord, we should tell the people to go away now, so that they can buy food in the nearby villages."

But Jesus said, "Why don't we feed them here?"

Now, the disciples had counted, and knew that there were about five thousand people sitting on the ground, waiting to see what Jesus would do next. They went among them to see if anyone had brought food.

And there was one boy who had a basket with his lunch in it. There were five small loaves, each not much bigger than a roll, and two little cooked fish.

"This is all the food there is, Lord," said the disciples. Jesus took up the basket and blessed the food, giving thanks to God for it.

"Take the basket and feed all the people," he said.

All the people? thought the disciples. There's hardly enough here to feed one!

Still, the disciples did as they were told and took the basket to the first row of people. All the people ate as much as they wanted—and yet there was still enough in the basket to feed the next row, and the next.

So it went on, until all five thousand people had eaten well from five small loaves and two little fishes. And there was still enough food left to fill twelve baskets!

IS IT A GHOST?

Some of the miracles that Jesus did, like healing illnesses, can now be done by science and medicine. We may feel that there is no more need for miracles. After all, people have even walked on the moon. But no one has yet walked on water—and that's exactly what Jesus did.

After Jesus had fed the crowds on the shores of Galilee, he was afraid that the people would force him to become their king. And that was not what he wanted. So he went away up the mountainside by himself to pray, and the disciples went on board a ship and waited for him on the lake.

And in the middle of the night, they saw someone walking across the water toward the ship, in the dark. They were terrified. "Is it a ghost?" they asked.

But Jesus called to them, "Don't be afraid. It's me, Jesus."

And Peter said, "Is it really you? Call me to come to you across the water."

"Come," said Jesus.

So Peter stepped off the side of the ship and started to walk to Jesus across the lake. The disciples hung over the side of the ship, open-mouthed at the sight of an ordinary man like them—their old friend Peter—acting like Jesus and doing the impossible.

Peter was just as surprised as they were. Imagine what it must have felt like skimming over the water, breaking all the laws of nature. But after a few steps Peter looked down and saw the deep waters of Galilee under his feet. He became afraid, and as soon as he was afraid, he started to sink.

"Help! Save me, Lord!" he cried.

And Jesus took him by the hand and led him across the waves and safely back on to the ship.

"You shouldn't have been afraid," he said.

And the disciples fell at Jesus' feet and worshiped him.

"You really are the son of God," they said.

REMOTE CONTROL

*We are used to doing things at a distance. We can contact people
in other countries by phone, e-mail, and the Internet. But at the time
when Jesus lived, there were no such devices—in fact, they would have
seemed like miracles themselves. In this story what struck people
as miraculous was not the healing of an illness, but the fact
that Jesus wasn't even there when it happened.*

At the time of Jesus, the Romans were in charge in Israel. They had a governor and an army stationed there.

There was a high-ranking Roman soldier in Capernaum whose favorite servant was ill and close to death. He had heard about Jesus and was absolutely sure that this Jewish healer could make his servant better. But he also knew that it might cause trouble if Jesus was seen entering a Roman soldier's house.

He sent a message to Jesus, telling him his problem. Some friends came to Jesus and said, "You should help this Roman. He is a good man and he has been kind to us Jews."

So Jesus set out toward the soldier's house. But before Jesus reached him, the soldier sent another message, saying, "There is no need for you to come to my house. I know what it is to give orders and to be obeyed. If I tell a man to do something, he does it. All you need to do is say that my servant will get better, and I know he will."

Jesus was amazed. He said to his followers, "This Roman has more faith than any of my fellow Jews. He believes I can heal his servant without even seeing or touching him."

And when the soldier's messenger got back to the house, he found that the servant who had been on the verge of death was sitting up in bed, looking perfectly well again.

Jesus had cured him from a distance, just as the Roman soldier had believed he would.

SAYING THANK YOU

*Leprosy is a terrible disease that destroys people's flesh.
It has been very nearly wiped out in the world today,
but in Jesus' time it was still very common—and
incurable. People were scared of lepers because
it was thought that leprosy was easily caught.
Lepers were made to keep away from healthy people
and to live on their own in special colonies.*

Jesus was walking to Jerusalem when he saw a group of ten lepers. They called out to him from a distance, "Jesus, Master, have mercy on us!"

Of course, Jesus knew what they wanted. "Go and show yourselves to the priests," he said.

And as the ten lepers turned to go, they found that their disease had disappeared and their flesh was healed. How happy they were! Now they could live a normal life among other people, return to their families, and hug their wives and children. No longer would people run away when they saw them in the street.

One of the ten turned back and fell to his knees before Jesus. "Thank you, thank you, Lord," he said. "God be praised for what you have done for me!"

Jesus looked surprised. "I thought ten of you were cured," he said. "Where are the other nine?"

Then he lifted the man to his feet and said, "Never mind, go on your way. Your belief in God has made you better."

BACK FROM the DEAD

*Have you ever known anyone who died? Death is so final that
we find it very difficult to come to terms with. We wish that
the dead person could be brought back to life. Jesus' last miracle
involving another person made that wish a reality.*

By now Jesus had performed so many miracles that everyone
was talking about him. Many of the Jews didn't like people
believing that Jesus was the son of God. They thought it would
cause trouble with the Romans. And the Romans thought Jesus
was a dangerous man.

So Jesus kept well out of the way of people in power, because
he knew they would use the smallest excuse to have him arrested
and put to death. He and his disciples left Judaea and crossed over
the river Jordan.

But while they were there, Jesus heard some bad news. He
was great friends with a man called Lazarus and his two sisters,
Martha and Mary. The women sent Jesus a message that Lazarus
was very ill.

Jesus waited two days, then said to the disciples, "Let's go back
to Judaea."

"It isn't safe, Lord," said the disciples. "You will be killed if you
return there."

"My friend Lazarus is asleep," said Jesus.

"Well, if he's only asleep, you needn't go to him," said the
disciples.

"I mean that Lazarus is dead," said Jesus. "And I'm glad we
weren't there, because now I can really teach you to believe."

Then the disciples agreed to go back with him, even though they
all knew that they might be in danger for being Jesus' friends.

When they got to Lazarus' house in Bethany, near Jerusalem, they found that the dead man had been in his tomb for four days.

Martha came out to greet Jesus, but Mary stayed in the house. Martha said, "If you had been here, my brother would not have died." And then she said, "Even now, if you ask God, I think he will do what you ask."

Jesus said, "Do you believe that I am the son of God?"

And Martha replied, "Yes, Lord."

Then she ran to her sister, Mary, and they both went with Jesus to Lazarus' tomb. On the way Jesus wept for the death of his friend.

The tomb was a cave with a big rock rolled in front to make a door. Jesus told his disciples to roll the stone away.

Martha said, "Lord, our brother has been dead four days—his body will stink."

And Jesus said, "If you believe, you will see the glory of God." Then he prayed to God and called in a loud voice, "Come out, Lazarus!"

And Lazarus, who had been dead, stepped out of the cave, still wrapped in his grave clothes. Jesus had performed his greatest miracle.

But from then on the rumors spread, and it was only a few weeks before Jesus was arrested and put to death. And three days later, he too rose from the grave and visited his disciples again. It is this central miracle of Jesus' life that Christians believe him to be the son of God.

ABOUT the STORIES

*If you want to read about any of these miracles
in the Bible, this is where to look them up:*

WATER INTO WINE *(The Marriage at Cana)*

This is found only in John 2:1–11. John makes a point of saying
that it was the first miracle of Jesus' ministry.

A NETFUL OF FISH *(The Miraculous Draft of Fishes)*

Luke 5:1–11. In John 21:1–14 the miracle takes place after
the Resurrection.

WEATHERMASTER *(Stilling the Storm)*

Matthew 8:23–27; Luke 8:22–25; Mark 4:35–41.

THROUGH THE ROOF *(The Man Cured of Palsy)*

Mark 2:1–12; Luke 5:17–26

THE BIGGEST PICNIC IN THE WORLD
(Feeding the Five Thousand)

This miracle can be found in all four Gospels. In Matthew
and Mark it takes place just after the death of John the Baptist.
There are similar accounts of Jesus feeding four thousand people
in Matthew 14:15–21; Mark 6:32–44; Luke 9:12–17; and John
6:5–14.

IS IT A GHOST? *(Walking on the Water)*

Mark 6:45–52; Matthew 14:22–33; John 6:15–21.

REMOTE CONTROL *(The Centurion's Servant)*

Matthew 8:5–13; Luke 7:1–10.

SAYING THANK YOU *(The Ten Lepers)*

Luke 17:11–19.

BACK FROM THE DEAD *(The Raising of Lazarus)*

Jesus also raised Jairus' daughter and at least one other person
from the dead. But John makes it very clear how this final miracle
led to Jesus' own death, in John 11:1–46.